A HISTORY of SIGHTINGS
— of the —
NIGHT PARROT
POLYGONICUS INCONSPICUUS NOCTURNUS

The elusive Bearded Night Parrot has achieved legendary status. Recent near-sightings have inspired twitchers scientists and ornithodontists worldwide to renewed efforts to make the much sought after confirmed sighting, or run over one.
Of these, Uncle Kev, former professor of Hydraulics at Northern Commando Training Academy, holds the current record for 'confirmed non-sightings and near-misses' and is founder member of the infamous Parraville Mouth-Organ Orchestra. (YMOO).

Broome

Earliest known sighting of N.P.
(5AM, Thurs, 14th Sept.)

x 'Very late Afternoon Parrot' seen, early evening 1867

Night Parrot
3AM, 30th Feb, 1947
Last known sighting:

x ←

← Tracks of the legendary 'Dotted White Lion' (a major predator of the BNP)

KEEP LEFT

CAUTION LOW SIGN

Kata Tjuta   Uluru

Neat Parrot flock seen flying in straight rows

Burke & Wills' camel bitten by Night Parrot →

Mr. Sturt turned back by 'Dotted White Lion'

1948
Skite Parrot heard bragging about size of bill (at 'Budgies in the Park' restaurant)

↑ Where the Great Australian Bighted (Bit)

Bight Parrot shadow found, 1910 →

Bright Parrot sighted in headlights, August 1963

The Edge

Cape Arid

Pezoporus Occidentalis:
a very secretive bird

All the WAY to W.A.

URGENT URGENT URGENT URGENT URGENT

UNCLE KEV MISSING

Renowned lobotanist, inventor and ex-commando Uncle Kev is reported missing on a mission to find the fabled Bearded Night Parrot. Declared a Living Legend for his devil-may-care approach to danger, he is famed for his ability to survive the most preposterous predicaments.

His family has mounted a huge search, and is confident he is alive and they will find him. "He always carries his 'TAIT'S' GPS," his sister said today. Ex-Commando sources have expressed concern, however. "There's a saying in the Force: 'He who has a Tait's is lost,'" an old fellow who did not want to be named said today. "They can be unreliable if not fully wound. Up to 360° out," he said.

MISSIN' ON MISSION Uncle Kev at the ex-commando ball in 2010. He is on leave from his job as Security Officer at the Ucranium Mine.

For Kaye Keck

When we heard about Uncle Kev, we hopped straight on the train across the vast Nullarbor Plain to rescue him.

All the WAY to W.A.

Our Search for Uncle Kev

Roland Harvey

Uncle Kev

Bearded Night Parrot

BACK

ALLEN&UNWIN

GREAT AUSTRALIAN BIGHT

At a secret location on the Great South Coast, we found our first exciting clue — a single dropping from the 'extinct' Bearded Night Parrot. We took this as a Sign that we were already hot on the trail.

Someone yelled, 'Whales ahoy!' so we climbed out to the viewing platform, where the whales can watch people.

We found a cooking pot and the remains of scorpion curry. The curry was still hot... Uncle Kev couldn't be far ahead!

KALGOORLIE

We checked out Uncle Kev's quarry, dug in 1953 with the help of his friend Hugh Jarms. There was a rumour that the wicked Budgie Smugglers Society had been spotted in the area, but we didn't see anything unsavoury.

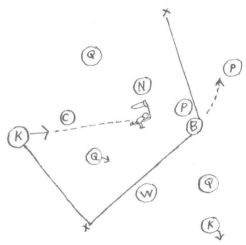

Uncle K Ⓚ put out bait Ⓑ in the form of succulent seeds dyed black to attract a bird of the night.

Trip wire Ⓦ alerted K Ⓚ to the bird's presence Ⓟ and he was shot by catapult Ⓒ carrying net Ⓝ.

Could Uncle Kev have found his quarry Ⓠ already, when we are only at the start of the book?

FREMANTLE

At the museum, a guard saw Henry making an exhibition of himself and threw him out.

We met an artist with a pet budgie, but he was of the opinion that the Night Parrot was probably just a budgie with a head-torch.

Penny had a Titanic moment on the submarine Uncle Kev used to command in his airforce days.

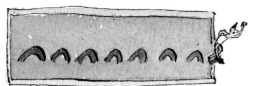

A photo in an exhibit at the musuem gave us a clue to Uncle Kev's movements.

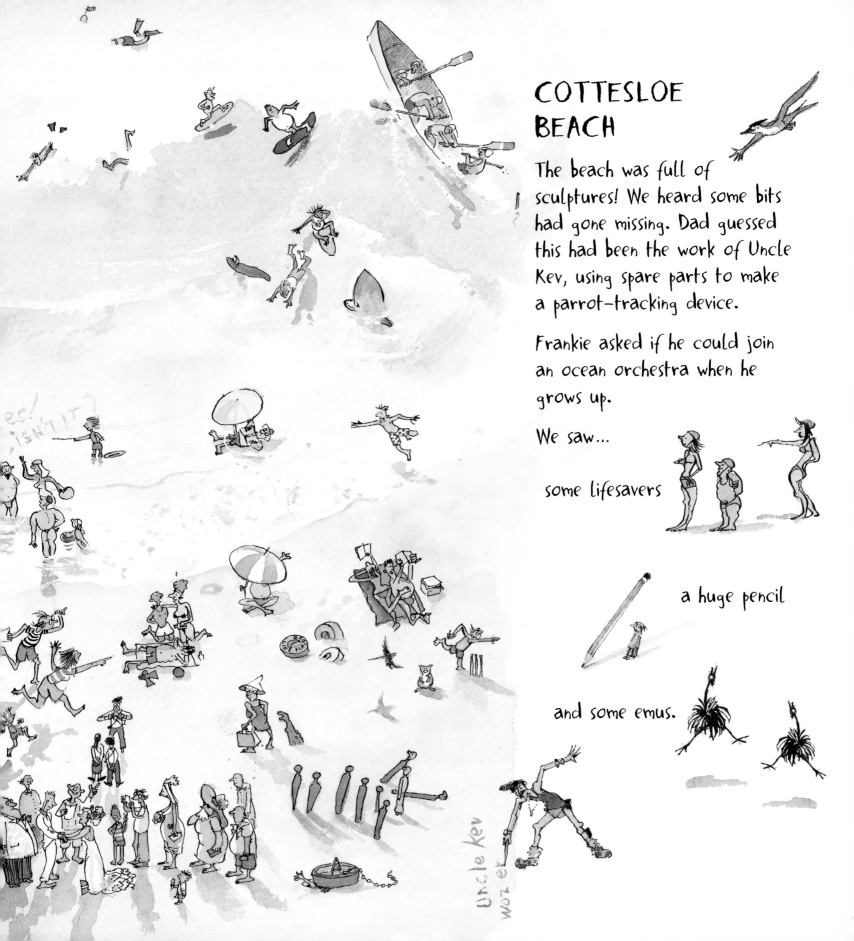

COTTESLOE BEACH

The beach was full of sculptures! We heard some bits had gone missing. Dad guessed this had been the work of Uncle Kev, using spare parts to make a parrot-tracking device.

Frankie asked if he could join an ocean orchestra when he grows up.

We saw...

some lifesavers

a huge pencil

and some emus.

WRECK OF THE BATAVIA

We followed Uncle Kev's trail to a low limestone island off the coast.

As it struck twelve that night, a terrible noise erupted outside our tent. Bones clanked, steel clashed and tortured souls shrieked...It was Dad, falling into the camping box.

Mum told us stories about the emu holding up the sky so we could go back to sleep. Frankie dreamed about sharks and dolphins, clear water and ancient pirate ships...

We found a pile of broken bricks...Could Uncle Kev have been practising his karate?

MONKEY MIA

We didn't see any monkeys or any mias but we fed bottle-nosed dolphins and lots of pelicans. A fish bit Frankie's finger, and he said he'd catch chips next time, too.

Mum's bottom... lip got sunburnt and Penny felt certain Uncle Kev was nearby, but we couldn't see him or any birds. We left seeds on the water just in case.

A dolphin did a pike with a double jackknife. Only Uncle Kev could have taught it that.

NINGALOO REEF

Henry saw 500 species of tropical fish.

Penny saw 220 species of coral and some very big fish, but we didn't see the whale sharks everyone was talking about.

Mum and Henry went out kayaking, and in the distance we thought we could hear Uncle Kev's creaky old pedal submarine, so off we went again.

A broken rubber band from Uncle Kev's submarine told us we were on the right track!

KARIJINI NATIONAL PARK

At an amazing gorge we helped people make a holiday video and discovered that Henry can climb vertical rock cliffs!

Apart from Uncle Kev's wallet, and a note and an arrow, he left no clue to which way he had gone...

We found Uncle Kev's special north-finding compass – STILL POINTING NORTH!!! Cleverly, we headed off to the north-east...

THE PILBARA

On the road, Dad was worried we'd get bored so he made us activity sheets. But we were too busy drawing stuff and identifying tracks and poo and flowers and extinct species, so we had to do our sheets after dinner.

Dad got right into his bush tucker guidebook. So far he has eaten green ants, poisonous seeds and worm castings. We collected 17 different feathers, including one from a wedgie-tailed eagle. Penny spotted 17 different animal tracks, including a Pilbara lizard, and Dad got 17 different insect bites. Mum collected a bag of gemstones to polish, and Henry made 17 different colours by grinding clay into powder to make paint.

We saw 17 million budgies but no Uncle Kev.

Night Parrot, daytime

MARBLE BAR

At the Hottest Place on Earth it is over 37.8 degrees for 154 days of the year. Blue-tongue lizards and goannas and frill-necked lizards don't mind, but people can melt, especially if they're softish and a bit runny to start with. The rock is just grey, but when you wet it the colours really shine.

Dad cooked dinner on a rock and Mum made her special giant bonnet omelette, the Om.

On a rock, we found a solar-powered moustache-trimmer. We were HOT!

BROOME

At Cable Beach, we went out on a boat to watch the sunset.

We didn't see any Night Parrots, but we did see an Aussie camel and some wise men. Mum thought the wise women were all out on another boat, fishing for dinner.

We saw a bird that weighs less than a handful of cornflakes and flies 600 million kilometres from southern Australia to Siberia each year. (It is further on the way back, because it is in miles.)

Winter plumage

FITZROY CROSSING

We were watching the footy at Fitzroy, starting to wonder if the naughty Night Parrot really existed, when a man who looked a bit like Uncle Kev's twin cousin came out of nowhere and kicked a heroic goal for the away team.

He had to leave before we got to speak to him...

So we all played kick-to-kick, and Frankie made a new friend.

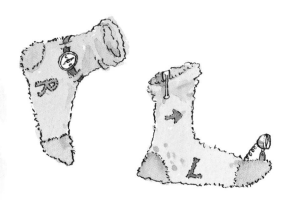

We found Uncle Kev's lucky socks, running across the oval.

PURNULULU NATIONAL PARK

We hired a gyrocopter in the Bungle Bungles. The hirogyro man said someone had borrowed a 'copter yesterday, looking for some bird...

Were we getting close, or was this just another bungle?

We found some gyro-droppings:

Uncle Kev's sardinofone,

mo-wax,

favourite book

and Swiss Army everything.

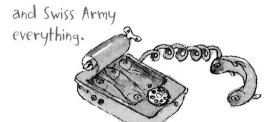

WYNDHAM

Right up north there were birds EVERYWHERE: darters, jabiru, Olga the brolga, and rainbow bee-eaters. We were so distracted we almost missed vital clues: a guide in a wooden canoe... another dropping... a lot of crocodiles and...

LOOK OUT, UNCLE KEV!

We found a Tait's GPS ticking inside a crocodile. He was swimming around in circles...

We couldn't believe it. There, before our eyes, were Uncle Kev and his Night Parrot...wait, his two Night Parrots!

Uncle Kev introduced the one without the beard to the one with a beard, and happily set them free. What a trip!

Come with us on our other family adventures!

First published in 2011

Copyright © Roland Harvey 2011

Allen & Unwin
83 Alexander Street
Crows Nest NSW 2065
Australia
Phone: (61 2) 8425 0100
Fax: (61 2) 9906 2218
Email: info@allenandunwin.com
Web: www.allenandunwin.com

A Cataloguing-in-Publication entry is available from
the National Library of Australia
www.trove.nla.gov.au

ISBN 978 1 74175 885 6

Illustration technique: dip pen and ink; watercolour
Designed by Roland Harvey and Sandra Nobes
Typeset in Harvey, created by Sandra Nobes from Roland Harvey's handwriting
Colour reproduction by Splitting Image, Clayton, Victoria
This book was printed in July 2011 at Tien Wah Press (PTE) Limited,
4 Pandan Crescent, Singapore 128475

1 3 5 7 9 10 8 6 4 2

Broome sweeps Night Parrot myth out door →

Uncertain sighting... 'Might Parrot' ↘

Sighting of large Wombat-shaped bird now thought to be Not Parrot...

Port Hedland

● Largest dot in W.A.

× Karratha

↙ Night Parrot Recipe Book found in Op-Shop.

Exmouth ×

Ningaloo Reef

× Goodnight Parrot last seen about 9.30 PM (in pyjamas)

Menu at o Marble Bar roadhouse shows 'Night Parrot Soup' (1963)

1922 × Search for Beakless Night Parrot succeeds.

1674 : Night Pirate wrecked on Dirk Hartog Is. ↓

o Carnarvon

Monkey Mia

Polite Parrot leaves last remaining seeds for others. ↓ ×

Near-sighting: Newt Parrot →

← Night-Before-Christmas Parrot seen 24 December 1942. Not a creature was stirring.

'Batavia' wrecked × ×× Kalbarri

Night Parrot poo found in midnight snack mixed with pumpkin seeds. →

Kite Parrot

Knight Parrot statue, Koolyanobbing

Kalgoorlie Boulder ↓ ×

Nerd Parrot seen on internet all night → ×

2 AM : Night Parent sees young bird at disco. ↓

West Coast NP on endangered list

× Perth

Last remaining Bite Parrot taken by Great Night Shark (or 'Night Pointer') →

1971: False sighting; Fremantle Arts Centre. Identified as Night Pirouette.

Tonight Parrot seen - late afternoon ↑

Nightie Parrot found down back of drawers → Albany ×

FEB 18 2014